Step by Step
Christmas Crèche

Leena Lane and
Gillian Chapman

This is what to do:
To make Mary

"Greetings, Mary!"

says an angel.

"God has chosen you!

Listen now, don't be afraid;

I'll tell you what to do.

You'll have a baby,

God's own Son.

Name him Jesus:

the Holy One."

You will need:

Long chenille stems

Scraps of colored fabric

Yarn

Small wooden beads, ¾" long

Color index card

Ruler

Scissors

Glue

Tape

Black felt-tipped marker

1
Bend a chenille stick in half to make the body.

2
Push a second chenille stick through the two halves to make the arms.

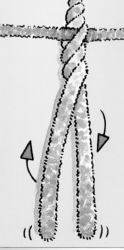

3
Twist the first chenille stick to secure the arms in place.

4

Fold each arm to meet the body and twist.

5

Glue a small bead onto the neck to make the head.

6

Wrap yarn around each arm. Secure the ends with glue.

7

Cut out a piece of index card 2³⁄₄" × 4".

8

Roll the cardstock around the body under the arms and secure with tape.

9

Draw a face with a black felt-tipped marker.

10

Cut out a rectangle of fabric 6¹⁄₄" × 2³⁄₈" and fold in half.

11

Cut a small slit across the fold, big enough to push the fabric down over the head.

12

Tie yarn around the waist to make a belt.

13

Cut out a triangle of fabric to make the headdress.

14

Glue the fabric to the head and where it touches the belt at the back.

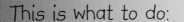

This is what to do:

To make Joseph and his donkey

Mary will be Joseph's wife.

He is good and kind.

Now they're going to Bethlehem.

Their donkey trots behind.

"How much farther?"

Mary sighs.

"Nearly there!"

Joseph replies.

You will need:

Long chenille sticks

Scraps of colored fabric

Scraps of felt

Yarn

Small wooden beads, ³/₄" long

Color index card

Brown thread

Tape

Small stick

Permanent ink black felt-tipped marker

Ruler

Scissors

Glue

To make Josep

1

Follow instructions I-II for Mary on pages 2 and 3, but draw a beard on the face with the black felt-tipped marker.

2

To make the overcoat, cut out a rectangle of felt 1¹/₈" × 5¹/₂". Fold in half and cut a slit down the center to the half-way point.

3

Place the fabric over Joseph's shoulders and tie yarn around the waist to make a belt. Pass the small stick through the loop in Joseph's arm to attach the staff. Complete by adding the head-dress as for Mary

To make the donkey

1

Bend a chenille stick into a basic animal shape.

2

Twist two more chenille sticks around the body to make pairs of legs.

3

Twist a smaller piece of chenille stick around the head to make the ears.

4

Cut several pieces of gray yarn and attach to the body using the chenille stick to make a tail.

5

Glue a bead onto the neck to make the head. Make sure the end of the chenille stick shows through the bead hole to make the nose. Draw on the eyes with the black felt-tipped marker.

6

Wrap gray yarn around the legs, body, neck, and ears to cover the chenille sticks. Wrap extra yarn around the body to make it fatter. Secure the ends with glue.

7

Cut a rectangle of brown felt 3¼" × 1½" for the saddle and glue to the donkey's back. Glue on other small pieces of felt to represent pieces of baggage.

8

Roll up a small rectangle of felt and tie with brown thread to make the blanket roll. Attach with glue.

This is what to do:

To make the innkeeper

The lamps are lit in Bethlehem.

It's been a busy day.

Mary and Joseph need a room.

They've walked a long, long way.

The inn is full, where can they sleep?

The stable's warm, so in they creep.

You will need:

Long chenille sticks

Scraps of colored fabric

Scraps of felt

Yarn

Small wooden beads, 3/4" long

Trimmings

Color index card

Ruler

Scissors

Glue

Tape

Small beads, buttons, or plastic lids

Black felt-tipped marker

1

Bend a chenille stick in half to make the body.

2

Push a second chenille stick through the two halves to make the arms.

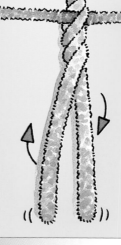

3

Twist the first chenille stick to secure the arms in place.

7

Cut out a piece of index card 2³⁄₄" x 2³⁄₈". Roll the cardstock around the body under the arms and secure with tape.

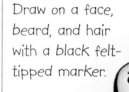

8

Draw on a face, beard, and hair with a black felt-tipped marker.

10

To make the apron, repeat step 9 using a smaller piece of fabric 4" x 1¹⁄₂", then tie yarn around the waist to make a belt.

11

Glue a small piece of chenille stick into the bead hole and push on small beads to make the hat.

Hats can be made from small beads, buttons, or small plastic lids. Use whatever you have available.

4

Fold each arm to meet the body and twist.

5

Glue a small bead onto the neck to make the head.

6

Wind colored yarn around each arm. Secure the ends with glue.

9

Cut out a rectangle of felt 6¹⁄₄" x 2³⁄₈", fold in half, and cut a small slit across the fold big enough to put the head through.

This is what to do:
To make the baby

Who is lying in the manger,
wrapped in blankets tight?
It's Jesus – Mary's special baby!
He was born this night.
Many people will hear of his birth –
God's own Son has come to earth.

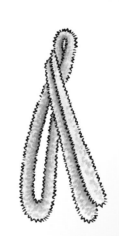

You will need:

Long chenille sticks
Scraps of white fabric
Scraps of white felt
Small wooden beads,
$1/2$" long
Scissors
Glue
Small box
Pieces of raffia
or straw
Black felt-tipped
marker

1
Bend a chenille
stem in half twice
to make the small
body and twist
together at one
end.

3

Draw on a face with the felt-tipped marker.

6

Wrap another length of fabric around the complete body, gluing it in place at the back.

7

Fill a small box with pieces of raffia or straw for the manger.

8

Place the baby inside the manger.

2

Glue a bead onto the neck to make the head.

4

Glue a small piece of white felt over the top of the head.

5

Wrap a small length of fabric around the top of the body, tucking in the head covering.

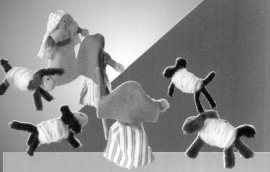

This is what to do:

To make the sheep and shepherds

Shepherds on the hills nearby

are guarding flocks of sheep.

The fire crackles and keeps them warm.

They must not fall asleep.

Wolves and lions prowl about.

The shepherds try to keep them out.

You will need:

Long chenille sticks

Scraps of colored fabric

Scraps of felt

Yarn

Small wooden beads, $^3/_4$" long

Trimmings

Color index card

Ruler

Scissors

Glue

Tape

Black felt-tipped marker

To make the shepherds

1

Use instructions for Mary on pages 2 and 3. Draw a beard on the face using the black felt-tipped marker.

2

Use different fabrics to make two or three more shepherds.

10

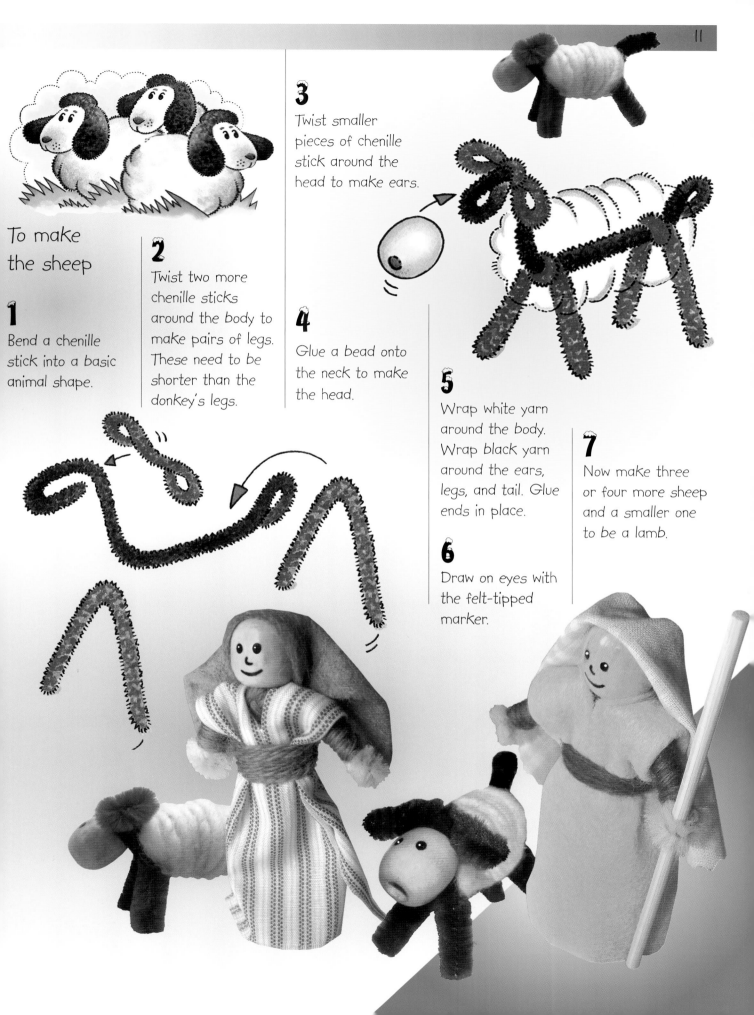

To make the sheep

1
Bend a chenille stick into a basic animal shape.

2
Twist two more chenille sticks around the body to make pairs of legs. These need to be shorter than the donkey's legs.

3
Twist smaller pieces of chenille stick around the head to make ears.

4
Glue a bead onto the neck to make the head.

5
Wrap white yarn around the body. Wrap black yarn around the ears, legs, and tail. Glue ends in place.

6
Draw on eyes with the felt-tipped marker.

7
Now make three or four more sheep and a smaller one to be a lamb.

This is what to do:

To make the angel

A blinding flash lights up the night:
an angel in the sky!
"Be not afraid! Your Savior's born
in Bethlehem nearby!
Go at once and find the place!"
The shepherds leap up and off they race.

You will need:

Long chenille sticks

Scraps of white fabric

Yarn

Small wooden bead,
$\frac{3}{4}$" long

Gold thread

Color index card

Ruler

Scissors

Glue

Tape

Black felt-tipped
marker

1

Bend a chenille stick in half to make the body.

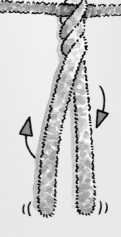

2

Push a second chenille stick through the two halves to make the arms. Twist the first chenille stick to secure the arms in place.

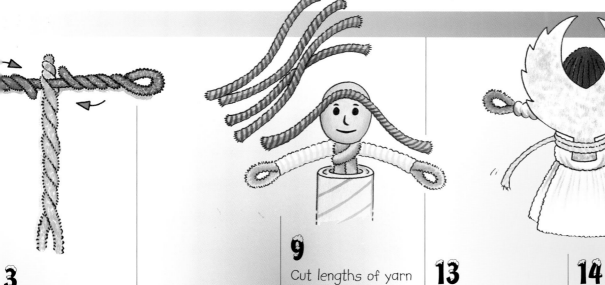

3
Fold each arm to meet the body and twist.

4
Glue a small bead onto the neck to make the head.

5
Wrap white yarn around each arm.

6
Cut out a piece of thin cardstock 2³/₄" × 2³/₈".

7
Roll the cardstock around the body under the arms and *secure with tape.*

8
Draw on a face with the *black felt-tipped marker.*

9
Cut lengths of yarn for the angel's hair. Begin at the front and glue them across the angel's head.

10
Cross the lengths of yarn over at the back to cover the whole head.

11
Cut out a rectangle of white fabric 6¹/₄" × 2³/₈" and fold in half.

12
Cut a slit across the fold and push fabric down over the angel's head.

13
Cut out wings from silver paper and glue to the back of the angel.

14
Tie gold thread around the waist to make a belt and secure the wings firmly in place.

This is what to do:

To make the stable and ox

The shepherds are looking in the town.

They run down every street.

The angel said he's in a manger,

the place where animals eat.

They try the stable – is he here?

Here is Jesus! They gather near.

You will need:

Large shoe box

Paints and brushes

Straw

Raffia

Twigs or lollypop sticks

Glue

Long chenille sticks

Small wooden bead, 3/4" long

Brown yarn

Black felt-tipped marker

To make the stable

1
Paint the inside and outside of the shoe box brown or yellow to make the stable.

2
Use the lid to make a sloping roof. Glue to the top of the box.

3
Tie pieces of straw or raffia together into bundles. Glue them to the roof.

4
Cover the outside walls with twigs or lolly pop sticks. Glue in place.

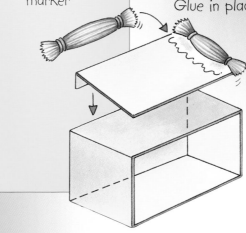

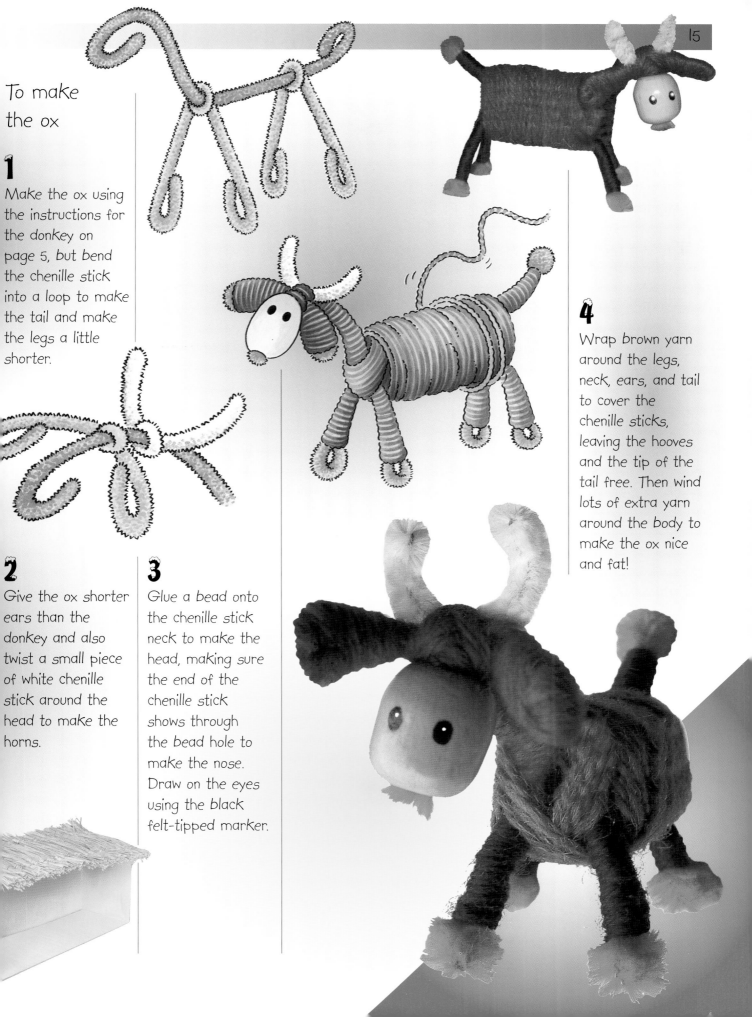

To make the ox

1

Make the ox using the instructions for the donkey on page 5, but bend the chenille stick into a loop to make the tail and make the legs a little shorter.

2

Give the ox shorter ears than the donkey and also twist a small piece of white chenille stick around the head to make the horns.

3

Glue a bead onto the chenille stick neck to make the head, making sure the end of the chenille stick shows through the bead hole to make the nose. Draw on the eyes using the black felt-tipped marker.

4

Wrap brown yarn around the legs, neck, ears, and tail to cover the chenille sticks, leaving the hooves and the tip of the tail free. Then wind lots of extra yarn around the body to make the ox nice and fat!

This is what to do:

To make the wise men and gifts

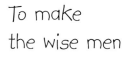

Far away in eastern lands,
wise men see a star.
"It means a new King has been born,
so we must travel far!"
They ride on camels day and night,
following the star so bright.

You will need:

Long chenille sticks

Scraps of colored fabric

Scraps of felt

Yarn

Gold thread

Small wooden beads, ³/₄" long

Colored thread

Trimmings

Color index card

Ruler

Scissors

Glue

Tape

Black felt-tipped marker

Small beads, buttons, or plastic lids

Shaped decorated beads or buttons

To make the wise men

1

All three men are made in the same way, just vary the colors of the fabrics. Use the basic figure instructions on pages 2 and 3 with the following slight variations.

2

ut out a rectangle f fabric 6¼" x ⅜", fold in half ngthwise. Cut a mall slit across e fold big enough put the head hrough.

3

Wrap a small strip of silky fabric or ribbon around the figure to make a shawl and tie the fabrics in place around the waist with the gold thread.

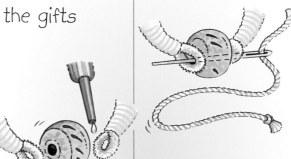

To make the gifts

2

Glue or sew the bead or button to the loops in the wise men's hands.

4

Draw on eyes, nose, and moustache with the black felt-tipped marker.

1

Beads and buttons come in all shapes and sizes. Choose three different shapes for the three wise men.

5

Make the beard with a small piece of black chenille stick. Push the ends into the top bead hole and glue the chenille stick around the face.

6

Glue on a small plastic lid, button, or bead to make the hat (see the innkeeper's instructions on page 7).

This is what to do:

To make the camels

The wise men see a palace
but they find no baby there.

"A new King?" asks King Herod.

"Tell me! I must prepare."

The wise men say they'll let him know.

Back to their camels, and off they go.

You will need:

Long chenille sticks

Scraps of colored felt

Colored yarn

Small wooden beads, ³/₄" long

Ruler

Scissors

Cotton ball

Black felt-tipped marker

Small beads and sequins

Glue

1

Make the basic animal shape from the chenille sticks, using the donkey instructions on page 5, but make the neck and legs longer.

2

Add in an extra piece of chenille stick to make the hump shape. Secure the ends of the hump where the legs twist around the body.

18

3

Twist a smaller piece of chenille stick around the head to make the ears using the donkey instructions.

4

Glue a bead onto the neck to make the head, and draw on the eyes using the black felt-tipped marker.

5

Wrap brown yarn around the neck, ears, and legs to cover up the chenille sticks. Leave the hooves and the tip of the tail free.

6

Pad out the hump with a cotton ball and wrap yarn around the body.

7

Cut out a rectangle of felt 1½" x 3" and glue the felt blanket onto the camel's back. Decorate the blanket with small beads and sequins.

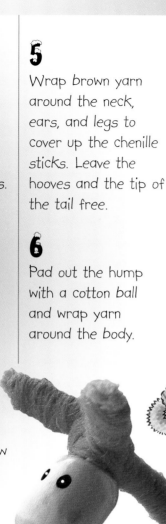

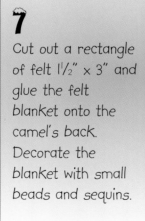

8

Now make two more camels using different colored yarns. Make their blankets in different colors and decorate them so each one is special.

This is what to do:

To make the trees and star

T he star has led them onwards
to a house in Bethlehem
Where Jesus and his mother
will be waiting there for them.
Fine gifts they bring for them to hold:
frankincense and myrrh and gold.

You will need:

Ruler

Pencil

Protractor

Scissors

2 sheets of paper

Gold foil card

Chenille sticks

Green felt

Brown yarn

Green index card

Modeling clay

Tape

Glue

To make the star

1

Draw two triangles measuring 4" x 4" x 4" out of the gold cardstock. Cut out and glue one over the other to make six-pointed star. Cut out the star shape from the gold foil card.

To make some trees

1

Twist two chenille sticks together to make a tree trunk.

2

Cut leaf shapes from green felt and twist onto the top of the tree trunk.

3

Wrap brown yarn around the tree trunk to cover up the chenille sticks.

4

Push tree trunk into a blob of modeling clay.

5

Cut a long strip out of green index card. Make the top edge jagged to look like grass.

6

Wrap the green cardstock strip around the clay base to hide it. Secure with tape or glue.

7

Make several more trees, all different sizes.

Everyone who sees the baby
worships him with joy.
Mary thanks and praises God
for her precious baby boy.
Shepherds, wise men, and angels sing
to Jesus their Savior,
the newborn King,

This is what to do:

To make the nativity crèche scene

1
The main scene will be the stable with ox, donkey, and manger, with trees around. Put Mary and Joseph in the stable on Christmas Eve.

2
The angel could be on the hillside outside Bethlehem where the shepherds are.

3
The star appears when Jesus is born. Place the star on the stable roof and Jesus in the manger ready for Christmas Day.

4
The shepherds come with some of their sheep early on Christmas morning. They are so excited, the innkeeper comes to see too!

5
The wise men see the star in the sky and travel to Bethlehem. They arrive much later and offer their gifts to Jesus. The wise men should be added to the scene at Epiphany on January 6.

Published in the United States of America
by Abingdon Press

Published in the UK
by The Bible Reading Fellowship

ISBN 0-687-06257-8

First edition 2004
U.S. edition 2005

Copyright © 2004 Anno Domini Publishing Services
1 Churchgates, The Wilderness,
Berkhamsted, Herts, HP4 2UB

Bible story copyright © 2004
AD Publishing Services Ltd, Leena Lane
Text and illustrations copyright © 2004
Gillian Chapman

Editorial Director Annette Reynolds
Project Editor Leena Lane
Art Director Gerald Rogers
Pre-production Krystyna Hewitt
Production John Laister

05 06 07 08 09 10 11 12 13 14—10 9 8 7 6 5 4 3 2 1

Printed and bound in Singapore

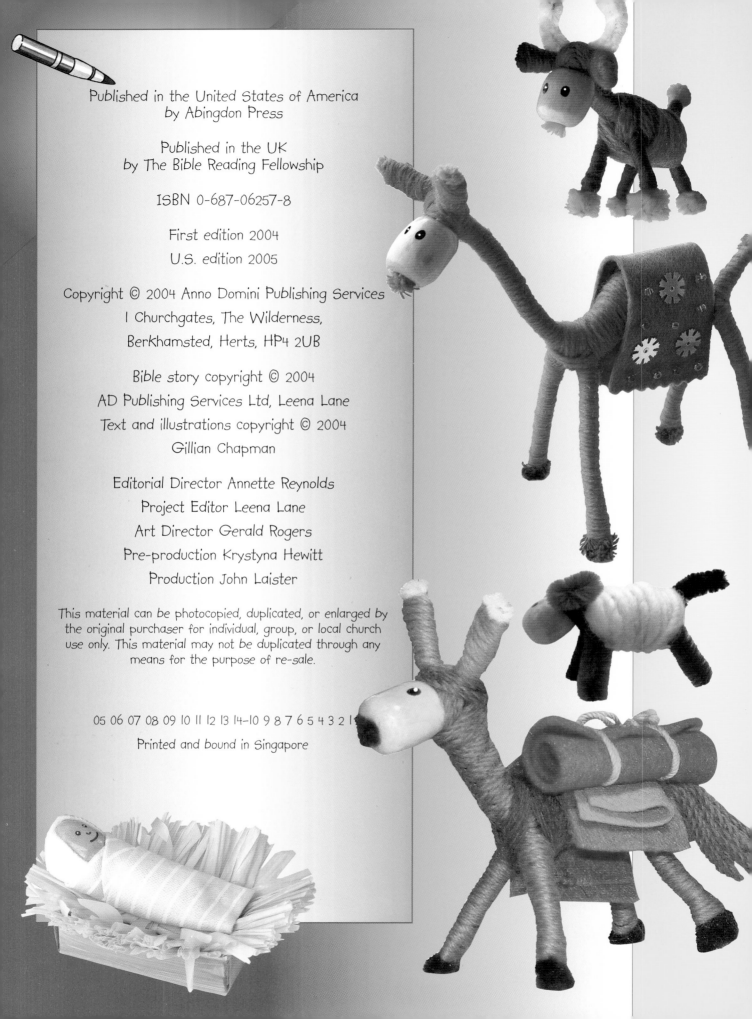